Because Your Mommy Loves You

by **Andrew Clements**   Illustrated by **R. W. Alley**

CLARION BOOKS
Houghton Mifflin Harcourt
Boston • New York • 2012

Clarion Books
215 Park Avenue South
New York, New York 10003

Clarion Books is an imprint of Houghton Mifflin Harcourt Publishing Company.

www.hmhbooks.com

The text of this book was set in 19-point Billy Serif.
The illustrations were executed in ink, watercolor, and acrylic.

Library of Congress Cataloging-in-Publication Data is available.
LCCN 2011025594

Manufactured in China
LEO 10 9 8 7 6 5 4 3 2 1
4500333883

For Kathy Brault, a dear friend and a great mom
—A.C.

For Zoë, are our kids lucky or what?
—R.W.A.

WHEN you get lost in the camping store, and you call out,

Mommy!

your mommy could say,
It's all right, I'm coming to find you!
But she doesn't.

She calls your name,

and you follow the sound of her voice.

When you find her, you get a big hug—
after you promise not to wander off again.

When the pack on your back
feels like a giant rock,

your mommy could say,
That looks awfully heavy
for you. Here, I'll carry it!
But she doesn't.

You both sit down a while
and share some water
and a handful of raisins.

Then she helps you strap on
your pack again,
and up the trail you go.

When you have to cross the stream,
and the log looks skinny and wobbly,

your mommy could say,
Don't worry, I'll take you across.
But she doesn't.

She goes over first to show you how.
And then you follow, all by yourself.

When you find a blueberry patch,
and it takes forever to fill one tiny cup,

your mommy could say,
Oh, don't bother—you've
done plenty.
But she doesn't.

She shows you where to find the best bushes,
and how to use your hat like a bowl.
And soon you have enough to make
blueberry pancakes.

When it's time to set up the tent,
and your side gets all tangled up,

your mommy could say,
This is a job for a grownup—let me fix it for you.
But she doesn't.

She shows you the pictures again. Then, step by step,
the poles and cloth and rope become . . .

When your marshmallow gets too close to the fire
and turns into a lump of charcoal,

your mommy could say,
What a shame!
Here, I'll make you
one that's just right.
But she doesn't.

She helps you find a stick shaped like a Y.
She shows you how to push it into the ground
beside the fire.
And your next marshmallow
is toasty-licious!

When the fire burns low,
and you see five shooting stars,
and it gets so cold you start to shiver,

your mommy could say,
Stay right there—I'll get you something cozy.
But she doesn't.

She hands you a flashlight
and reminds you where
you left your sweatshirt.

You go into the dark tent,

and after you find it,
you pull it on
and hurry back to the fire.

And the two of you
snuggle extra close.

When it's very late,
and you can barely keep your eyes open,

your mommy could say,
You're all tuckered out. Let me carry you to bed.
But she doesn't.

She pulls you up,
and you help her put out the fire.
She follows you to the tent,
and you crawl in first.

While you take your boots off,
she fluffs up your pillow
and unrolls your sleeping bag.
You slide inside,

and she zips the zipper up to your chin.

And then your mommy could say,
See you when the sun comes up!

or

Lots more hiking tomorrow!

or

Get a good rest, now!

But she doesn't.

She whispers,

I love you.